Lost in
the Storm

Lost in the Storm

by Holly Webb
Illustrated by Sophy Williams

tiger tales

tiger tales

5 River Road, Suite 128, Wilton, CT 06897
Published in the United States 2017
Originally published in Great Britain 2007
by the Little Tiger Group
Text copyright © 2007 Holly Webb
Illustrations copyright © 2007 Sophy Williams
ISBN-13: 978-1-68010-410-3
ISBN-10: 1-68010-410-1
Printed in China
STP/1800/0128/0317
10 9 8 7 6 5 4 3 2 1

For more insight and activities, visit us at www.tigertalesbooks.com

Contents

For Tom

Chapter One
The Exciting Outdoors

Fluff the kitten was lying in her basket on her back, showing off her furry tummy and snoring a little. She wasn't deeply asleep, just dozing, with her paws tucked under her chin. Her little body only took up one corner of the basket. Fluff was getting bigger, just not very fast. The basket was in a patch of winter sunshine, and it was incredibly cozy. She was planning to spend as much of the afternoon as possible like this. She needed to keep her energy up, after all, for when Ella got home from school and wanted to play.

Ella's mom walked past, and Fluff opened one eye thoughtfully. Was there any chance of a snack? Ella's mom reached down to tickle her behind the ears. She hadn't wanted Ella to have a cat at first. When she and Ella first met Fluff at the farm where she'd been born, Mom had called Fluff a dirty, scruffy little kitten, and told Ella she could have a goldfish instead. (Fluff was a little sad that Ella didn't have a goldfish, actually. She would have liked one.) But when she'd seen how upset Ella was, and understood that

8

she really was old enough to take care of a kitten properly, she'd changed her mind. Now she fussed over Fluff almost as much as Ella did. Fluff purred at the attention and waved her paws idly. Ella's mom petted the silky fur on Fluff's tummy and laughed. She reached for the packet of cat treats on the counter. Fluff sprang out of her basket in half a second, standing on tiptoe with her paws against the cupboard door, scrambling to get closer.

"I shouldn't be doing this." Mom shook her head. "You eat way too many of these. You'll get too big for your basket."

Fluff delicately nibbled the salmon-flavored treat out of Mom's hand and pranced back to her basket. She knew Ella's mom was joking. The basket was huge! Fluff liked to lie up against one edge of it to make it seem smaller. She had a feeling that Ella and her dad had gone a little over the top in the pet store.

After Fluff had run away from the farm to escape being taken home by a horrible boy who wanted to feed her to the next-door neighbor's German shepherd, Ella and her family had finally found her again a couple of days before Christmas. It had been the snowiest Christmas in 20 years, so Ella hadn't been able to go out and buy Fluff a Christmas present. She'd made up for it when the snow melted, spending most of her Christmas money from Grandma on cat toys. Ella walked past a pet store on her way home from school, and she liked to stop in and spend her money on things for Fluff. Fluff didn't mind at all—she *really* liked those salmon-flavored cat treats....

Suddenly, Fluff pricked up her ears. She could hear someone opening the front door. Ella was back from school!

"I'm home!" Ella called, and Fluff bounded up to the front door to wind herself around Ella's legs lovingly. She enjoyed having a nice sniff of the outdoors, too, poking her nose around the edge of the door.

Ella scooped her up gently. "Hey! No running off, Fluff!"

Fluff rubbed her head up and down Ella's chin. She wasn't trying to run off. It would just be fun to go and wander around outside. She hadn't been allowed out much since Ella and her family had adopted her, and sometimes it could be a little bit boring being an indoor cat. Ella took her out in the yard on the weekends, but it was too dark when she got home from school. Fluff loved the yard, scratching the tree bark, chasing leaves, watching the bird feeder. She wished she could go and explore more when they were out, but she could see how worried Ella was about her getting lost again, so she stayed close by. Fluff thought it was a little silly, though—as if she could get lost just by investigating the yard next door! She'd only been lost before because she had been so young. She was bigger now, and she could find her way anywhere, she was sure.

"I brought you home a present!" Ella said, as she shut the door. She carried Fluff into the kitchen, gave her mom a quick hug, and started to dig around in her school bag.

"Another trip to the pet store?" Mom asked, half-annoyed, half-laughing. "That cat is going to think it's Christmas every day."

Ella looked a little guilty. The pet store was on her way home from school, and she was allowed to stop in, as long as she didn't take long. Mom liked to know where she was. "I know. But you did say she needed a collar. They haven't had any really nice ones before, but look at this!" She held up a bright blue leather collar. "Isn't it beautiful? And look, it has a place for her name and everything." She fastened it around Fluff's neck, and Fluff shook her head briskly, not sure about this new feeling.

"It's a bit big," Ella said, studying it thoughtfully. "But she'll grow into it, won't she? It looks so pretty." Dangling from the collar was a little round golden tag. "You could choose," Ella explained. "If I go back to the store, they can put her name on it. But I wanted to check what else we should put. Should we have our address engraved on it, too, in case she gets lost?"

Mom looked thoughtful for a moment. "Actually, I think just our phone number. Not even her name. I know it sounds silly, but if we put her name on, it means everyone knows it, and someone could call her over. We don't want anyone to find it easy to steal our beautiful kitten, do we?"

Ella looked horrified. "No! I didn't

16

think of that. Just the phone number then." She picked Fluff up again and held her tight, so tight that Fluff wriggled after a few seconds, trying to get down.

"Hey! Ella, it's okay. It's just a safety thing. It's really, really unlikely." Mom gave her an anxious look. "I know you love Fluff, and of course we don't want to lose her, but I think you're just worrying too much. Fluff is growing up now, and cats are very independent. I think you're going to have to let her out on her own soon."

Ella looked down at Fluff, who was now sniffing at the counter, hoping for more treats. "But what if she gets lost again?" she asked.

Mom sat down next to her. "There's

no reason why she should, Ella. Cats have a really good sense of direction. She won't just go running off for no reason. She'll look around, make sure she knows how to get back. She's clever, isn't she?"

Ella nodded. "Yes," she agreed, and then she added doubtfully, "but she was lost before."

"She was really young then, and it wasn't her fault, anyway. She'd never been away from the farm. And she found you, didn't she? That shows you just how amazing her instincts are."

"Mmm." It was true. They'd never understood how Fluff had found her way back to them, but Ella couldn't believe it was just a coincidence.

"I think we should get Dad to put a cat flap in the back door. Then Fluff will be able to come in and go out when she wants to."

"Okay," Ella agreed reluctantly, still anxiously eyeing Fluff. She was such a small kitten, even now that she'd grown a little bit—and even with her pudgy, cat-treat-filled tummy. Would she really be safe out on her own?

On the weekend, Ella's dad went with Ella to the pet store to buy Fluff a cat flap. It was the first time that Ella had been there and not enjoyed it. Normally she just wandered around wishing she had more money to buy presents for Fluff! Now she stared worriedly at the display of collars while Dad and the

pet store owner discussed different kinds of cat flaps. The engraved tag for Fluff's collar was ready for them to pick up, too, but Ella's excitement about it was almost gone. It had been replaced by a sense of relief that when Fluff went out of her new cat flap and disappeared, at least there was a chance that someone would find her and call.

The cat flap was a neat one that could be locked, or set so Fluff could only go through it one way. It was a pain to fit, though. Ella's dad had to saw a chunk out of the back door, and it took him a long time. When it was finally finished, Ella crouched on the lawn waving the salmon-flavored cat treats to tempt Fluff through. It didn't take her long to get the idea, although she looked very surprised when she first tried it. She had her front legs on the doorstep and her back legs in the kitchen, and she wasn't quite sure where her tummy was. She gave a panicked sort of wriggle, and suddenly all of her was in the yard. Fluff looked around suspiciously, not entirely sure how it had happened.

"Clever Fluff," Ella whispered, rewarding her with cat treats. "Do you like your new cat flap? You will be careful, though, won't you?" She scratched Fluff's favorite behind-the-ears spot. "You stay close to the yard." Ella gulped. "No running out into the road, Fluff!"

Fluff purred as Ella petted her. She wasn't sure she completely understood this cat-flap business yet, but it seemed to mean that she could just go out whenever she wanted to! And then get back in again for a nap in her basket—it sounded wonderful to her, but she could hear in Ella's voice that she wasn't completely happy about it. She rubbed herself all around Ella twice in a comforting way, making her giggle. *I won't run away*, she promised. *Don't worry.*

For the first few days, Fluff kept her expeditions confined to the yard. There was plenty to explore there anyway. Ella had a big yard, long and narrow. Her mom loved gardening, and there were big flowerbeds, which

Fluff wasn't too interested in, but also many exciting corners and pockets. Best of all was a tall old apple tree, its branches starting low to the ground. Ella had a swing in it, where she loved to sit and daydream. The apple tree was Fluff's first real chance to practice climbing, and it made a perfect claw-sharpener, too.

But after a little while, Fluff had found all the interesting things in her yard, and she scrambled up the fence to look down at the yard next door. She'd seen Mrs. Jones, Ella's neighbor, before. Ella had held Fluff up to the fence to be admired, and Mrs. Jones had commented on her beautiful markings. Fluff hadn't had a chance to see much of the yard, but now she noticed something very exciting. She plunged down the other side of the fence with an undignified scratch of claws, and stopped at the bottom for a calming lick of her ruffled fur. Then she set off to investigate. Mrs. Jones's yard had a pond! With fish in it, Fluff soon discovered.

She spent the rest of the afternoon perched on the rocks by the side of the water, dreamily watching the fish darting back and forth. Was it her imagination, or were they swimming slightly faster, looking a little more worried? Obviously she would need practice, but Fluff was fairly sure that if she dipped a paw in and held it still, she would be able to catch a fish....

Fluff was so interested in the fish that she almost forgot to get back to the house before Ella arrived home from school. She didn't want Ella to worry that she'd gotten lost, and, of course, she loved to see her. She could always tell when it was almost time for Ella to be back.

Fluff sprang up from her place on the rocks and scooted halfway up Mrs. Jones's fence before she'd even realized she was climbing. Then she almost slid backward and had to jab her claws in hard to stay on. Embarrassed, she flung herself up and over and streaked across the lawn to the cat flap. Ella was just coming in the front door, and Mom laughed as Fluff shot through the flap.

"Just in time, Fluff! Oh, you're all out of breath."

Fluff glared up at her, and sat down in the middle of the kitchen floor, curling her tail around her legs in a dignified pose. She was trying not to look like a kitten who'd almost fallen off a fence, but her whiskers were still twitchy with excitement. Outside might be a little dangerous, but she loved it!

Chapter Two
A Flurry of Snow

It was mid-February, and it had suddenly gotten cold again. Ella was extra-glad to have Fluff sleeping on her feet at night. Mom and Dad had said that she was supposed to sleep in her basket, but they pretended not to notice that actually she always curled up with Ella. Mostly she stayed at the end of the bed, but a couple of times Ella had gone to sleep cuddling her, and Fluff slept snuggled under her chin.

Ella woke up early that morning. The comforter was huddled up around her shoulders where she'd wriggled herself down in the cold during the night. Fluff was pacing up and down the windowsill, meowing excitedly.

"Fluff!" Ella moaned. "The sun is barely up yet. What's the matter?" Then she sat up, confused. It was almost light, but the room looked different somehow. And why was Fluff making such a big deal? Ella wrapped the comforter around her shoulders and padded over to the window.

"Oh, wow! It snowed again!" she exclaimed as she peered out.

It had snowed very heavily just before Christmas, when Fluff was lost, but the cold snap hadn't lasted long. January had just been gray and wet.

"Why does it have to be a school day?" Ella sighed. "It'll be too dark to play outside after school."

Ella tried to argue at breakfast that school would probably be closed because of the snow, but Mom said it would have been announced on the radio. She promised faithfully to help Ella build an entire family of snowmen when she got back, and they dug out boots and scarves and hats for the walk. Ella usually walked on her own to school. It wasn't very far, and she met up with some of her friends, but today Mom said she'd go, too, at least most of the way, because she was worried Ella might slip over in the snow.

"Don't go out today, Fluff," Ella said, as she struggled to pull her boots on over two pairs of socks. "It's really cold, and the snow's very deep. You'd probably sink up to your whiskers. Stay in the house and keep nice and warm."

Fluff snuggled into her basket and snoozed for a while, but she was itching to go outside. Despite what Ella had said, Fluff really wanted to investigate the snow. She padded over to the cat flap and peered out. The snow was brand-new and inviting. She couldn't see any tracks in it, just a sheet of crunchy, sparkling white. She pushed open the cat flap gently with her nose and sniffed. The snow smelled so fresh, and she could hear the wind blowing through the trees, the snow falling from the branches with soft noises. How could she stay inside? She wouldn't go far....

Fluff eased herself out of the cat flap, shaking her paws daintily as they hit the snow. She knew all about snow, of course.

Her long journey from the farm to Ella's house had almost ended in disaster when she was caught in a snowstorm. But today she was just going for a quick look around. Nothing could go wrong. She'd explore the snowy yard, and as soon as she felt cold or tired, she could go back inside to warm up, and probably beg for some cat treats from Ella's mom. *Ella was just being too careful*, Fluff thought. It was nice that Ella wanted to take care of her, but really, she could take care of herself!

Fluff's paws sank deeply into the snow. It must have been snowing for most of the night, because there was a thick layer over everything. The yard looked completely different, covered in strange lumps where the plants had been. Fluff looked down and saw her paw prints in the snow—the only ones. It was very exciting to be the only animal outside. She gave a little jump to make more prints, scattering her tracks around the lawn in a pattern.

It was still snowing a little, the flakes drifting down idly, tickling Fluff's whiskers. She sat up on her back legs and tried to catch them with her front paws, but the snowflakes floated on the wind, and it was hard to tell where they were going. One particularly large flake came twirling down past Fluff's nose, and she waved her paws at it. It seemed to dance around her, so she twirled to chase it and suddenly she was flat on her tummy in the snow. Fluff stood up quickly, checking to see that no one had seen her slide. The snowflake had disappeared into the thousands of other snowflakes, and Fluff angrily spat snow out of her mouth. She set off across the yard to find something else to do.

Suddenly she noticed that hers weren't the only tracks anymore. A delicate pattern of forked prints was spattered over the snow by the fence. And perched on top of the fence, eyeing her cautiously, was a blackbird!

It whistled shrilly and hopped down into the yard next door. Fluff trotted along the path of tracks eagerly. She'd gotten the hang of walking in the snow again now, lifting her paws higher than usual. The tracks led underneath the fence, and Fluff wriggled after them, not even remembering that she'd planned to stay in her own yard. The blackbird was on the bird feeder now, gobbling breadcrumbs that had been put out. It must have been that morning, because Fluff could see the prints of Mrs. Jones's boots in the snow. She gazed hopefully up at the blackbird for a while, but it just squawked and chattered at her angrily. Clearly it didn't want to come down to be chased. She hopped from footprint to footprint instead and realized that Mrs. Jones must have gone down to check on the pond, too. Her prints led right up to the edge. Fluff stood in them and leaned over to look. The pond was frozen! She could see the water-plants poking out in places, snow drifted up around them, but most of the pond was covered with strange, clear, greenish ice. Fluff couldn't see the fish at all; they must be hiding at the bottom. Cautiously, she put a paw on the ice, and it skidded. She jumped back quickly. She'd already fallen over once, and the ice was incredibly cold.

The pond was close to Mrs. Jones's fence, and there was an inviting gap underneath. The yard next door smelled really interesting; somehow, the cold was making all the smells so much better! Fluff flattened herself to the ground and squirmed through the gap, her whiskers twitching excitedly. Then she squirmed some more, and then she wriggled. Then she stopped wriggling. She wasn't going anywhere. She was stuck!

Chapter Three
Fluff's Bird Chase

Fluff hunched her shoulders worriedly, trying to figure out what had gone wrong. The gap had looked perfectly big enough—her whiskers had fit through, so the rest of her should have been able to. Then she realized—it was her collar. It had caught on something, maybe a nail sticking out of the fence. Suddenly Fluff panicked and started to struggle, pulling backward and forward desperately, meowing frantically and scratching with her paws. She meowed for Ella to come and help her, forgetting that Ella was at school. But after a couple of minutes she was too exhausted to struggle any longer, and she slumped to the ground, her neck aching where the collar was pulling at her.

Fluff lay panting miserably, wondering what to do. She supposed she would just have to wait for someone to rescue her. When she didn't get home in time to meet Ella from school, they would start to worry, wouldn't they? Or maybe Mrs. Jones would come out to look at her pond again. Fluff shivered. It was going to be a long, cold wait.

Fluff meowed with frustration.

It was just so silly. Her collar was too big, and it had gotten caught. It wasn't her fault! She gave a furious wriggle, and suddenly she felt the collar stretch. Maybe instead of trying to pull the collar off the fence, she should be trying to get out of the collar altogether. She pulled downward, trying to stretch the collar even more. It hurt a little, but the collar did seem to give. Now if she could just pull herself backward....

Fluff popped out of the collar, feeling as though she might have pulled her ears off. She twitched them. No, they were still there. She'd done it! Feeling very proud of herself, she examined the collar. There wasn't a nail, just a sharp splinter of wood sticking out of the fence. Fluff hadn't been any farther than the yard next door on her travels before, so as she came out from under the fence she looked around carefully, trying to figure out if this was another cat's territory, or even worse, if there was a dog around. Everything smelled all right, but she wasn't sure how the snow changed smells, and she wanted to be extra cautious. As she sat watching, she noticed a strange metal thing in the middle of the yard, a pole, with things hanging from it. Fluff sat with her head to one side, trying to figure out what it might be. Suddenly, two birds flew down to perch on the hanging bits, and she realized it was full of birdseed. Fluff's ears pricked forward, and she sank into a hunting crouch. If only she could get closer.... Fluff hadn't had much opportunity to practice her hunting skills yet, but she was eager to learn. Her mother had tried to teach her how to catch mice back at the farm, but Fluff thought birds looked more fun to chase.

With a heavy thumping sound, a pair of enormous pigeons landed on the snowy grass. They were too big to perch on the feeders, but there were a few seeds and nuts scattered around in the snow underneath, and the pigeons started gobbling them up greedily.

Fluff's heart began to beat faster with excitement. This was her chance! How happy Ella would be if Fluff brought her back a pigeon! She left her hiding place and crawled closer on her tummy, low to the ground, her paws muffled by the snow. The pigeons completely ignored her, too busy making sure they didn't miss any seeds that might be half-buried in the snow. With a massive burst of energy, Fluff pounced, fastening her teeth into the tail of the nearest pigeon, which let out a loud squawk of surprise. She'd done it! She'd actually caught something!

The pigeon looked around, saw that it was being attacked by a cat in the middle of its lunch, and panicked. Okay, so it was only a very small cat, but then pigeons are known for having very small brains.

Squawking in terror, the pigeon tried to fly away, but this was a bit difficult with a cat attached to a vital part of its flying equipment. Fluff hung on as the wings beat up and down. Her first catch was *not* getting away. Seeing that flapping wasn't going to work, the pigeon changed its tactics and began to run *and* flap, trying to build up some speed to help lift itself off the ground. Kind of like a feathery plane thundering down the runway, it set off across the lawn. Fluff was dragged along behind like a water skier, her paws making tracks in the snow.

At last the pigeon managed enough lift and pulled itself off the ground with a mighty effort, taking Fluff with it. Her front paws left the ground, and she peered down worriedly. Surely the pigeon couldn't actually fly off with her.... There was no way she was going to let go! Luckily for Fluff, the tail gave up instead. A large clump of feathers came right out, and the pigeon flew off looking decidedly bald. It landed clumsily at the top of a nearby tree, and squawked abuse at Fluff, furiously preening its mangled tail. Fluff sat on the ground, panting and spitting feathers. *Did that count as catching a pigeon?* she wondered. Could she claim it as half a pigeon, maybe? She heaved a happy sigh and spat out a last feather.

Fluff gazed up at the pigeon, still angrily squawking at her, and noticed that it had started to snow again. She danced around the lawn, pouncing on the twirling snowflakes. This was so much fun! It was cold, of course, but her thick fur was keeping her cozy, and in a few minutes she would head back to her cat flap and the nice warm house. She ran around and around, flipping her tail, still full of excitement after her hunt. The snow was coming in big, thick flakes now, large enough to snap at with her teeth.

Fluff was enjoying herself so much that she didn't notice how heavy the snow was becoming. The pigeons and the other birds had disappeared, and it was terribly quiet. Fluff opened her mouth and tried to catch a particularly plump and dizzy snowflake, and then looked around in surprise. She couldn't see at all! The entire yard was a mass of whirling white and gray, and Fluff couldn't see anything beyond two whisker-lengths away. She shuddered. This was too much like her scary journey a couple of months before. She needed to get home at once. But—where was home? Fluff gulped. She couldn't even see the fence.

A gust of icy wind rushed at Fluff, and she felt as though it had blown right through her. Her ears were laid back against her head, and the snowflakes felt like stabbing needles as they blew into her fur.

Worriedly, she peered around her. She could just about see the tree that the pigeon had flown into, so the fence must be over there somewhere. Leaning into the wind, she plowed forward. It was so cold now! At last, there was the fence. Fluff's panicky feeling eased a little. She only had to get across the yard next door, and she would be home. She wriggled under the fence, and then followed her nose straight across. She was almost there—and once she was back home, she was *not* coming out again. Not until it stopped snowing, anyway.

Fluff almost bumped into the next fence, but she didn't mind; she was just so glad to see it. She popped out from underneath; she was back in her yard!

Except—this didn't look like her yard. Even with the snow everywhere, it didn't feel right. Ella's yard had several little walls and hedges and things, but this yard was big and flat. Had she miscounted the number of fences? Fluff didn't think she'd gone into another yard after the one two doors down, but maybe in the excitement of exploring, she had…?

Feeling frightened, she scurried across this strange yard to the next fence, hoping desperately that this time she would see somewhere she knew. The snow was drifting up against the fences now, and she had to half-burrow through. Hopefully, she pushed the snow out of the way with her nose and stared around. This yard was full of playground equipment—a slide and a little wooden house, half covered in snow. Fluff had never been here before.

Fluff had gone the wrong way in the storm—and now she was completely lost!

Chapter Four
A Cozy Shelter

Fluff stood still for a while, sniffing the air, hoping to catch a familiar scent that would lead her home. But the falling snow deadened the smells as well as the noises, and Fluff felt completely blind. What should she do? Had she gone past Ella's house in the storm somehow? Should she be going back or forward?

One thing was certain. She *had* to move somewhere. Sitting still wouldn't keep her warm. She could feel the cold seeping into her bones—even her whiskers ached with it. The awful thing was, she might be going even further away from home! Miserably, Fluff forced her paws to keep plodding on through the deep snow. Without realizing, she slipped through a gap in a broken-down old fence at the bottom of a yard, and strayed into the woods that ran along behind the houses on Ella's street. It was even harder going. She was wading through drifted snow under tall and menacing trees. Fluff knew she'd never been anywhere like this before, and it made her shudder. The trees seemed to wave their dark arms at her, and their roots tripped her up. It felt as though they did it on purpose, sending her rolling into hollows of deep snow so she had to struggle and fight her way out. Every time it happened, Fluff grew just a little bit more tired.

It was getting dark, and even harder to see. Fluff wished sadly that she had listened to Ella and never gone out in the snow. She still didn't quite understand how she had managed to get so lost. One minute she had known exactly where she was, and the next she'd had no idea. It had all happened so fast. Fluff shivered. There was nothing she could do about it now. She needed to rest, but where could she go? There were a few places under the trees, where the roots had made little burrows, but they didn't look very warm. Fluff needed somewhere out of the biting wind.

Suddenly, something loomed up out of the gloom. Fluff peered forward doubtfully. It certainly wasn't a tree. In fact, it looked more like a house.

With a fresh burst of energy, she trotted forward, picking her way carefully over the snow. It was a rundown old house, but it had been empty now for years and years. The door was boarded up, but there were plenty of holes where a small cat could creep in. Fluff sighed with relief as she squeezed herself between the boards. Even just inside the door the difference was wonderful—no more freezing wind slicing through her fur.

Staggering with tiredness, Fluff headed further in, looking for somewhere comfortable to sleep. Gratefully she spotted a pile of old blankets in one corner. They were smelly and stained, but Fluff wasn't feeling picky. She burrowed in, wanting to be as warm as possible, and hollowed herself out a little nest in the rags. She closed her eyes, wrapped her tail around her nose, and let a warm tide of sleep wash over her. All at once she was back home, with Ella, being petted, and fed cat treats.

But then she heard a noise. Fluff twitched in her sleep, fighting to stay in her happy dream. Oh, she didn't *want* to wake up, and be back in this cold, real adventure! Something was breaking into her dream—a meowing sound. Fluff sighed. It was no good; she wasn't asleep anymore. She poked her head up from her blanket nest and gazed around grumpily. She couldn't see anything, and the house was silent, except for the eerie shrieking of the wind outside. Was it that that she'd heard? It must have been. Fluff was just settling back down to sleep when she heard the meowing again.

Something was crying for help!

Ella rushed home—as fast as she could in slippery boots—full of news about her fun day. School had been all about snow—talking about snowflake patterns in science, writing snow poems in English, and lots and lots of playing outside in the snow at lunch and recess.

"We had an awesome snowball fight," Ella told her mom happily, as she watched her make a mug of hot chocolate. "Oooh, can I have marshmallows, please?" She took the hot chocolate and sat down, sipping it slowly. "Yum. It's so cold out there, Mom. My fingers are freezing, even though I had my gloves on." She gripped the warm mug tightly. "They're just now thawing out." Ella swallowed a big mouthful of hot chocolate and sighed happily. It was nice to be back inside. "It's so cool that it's Friday, and we have the entire weekend free. Can we go sledding in the park tomorrow?" Then she looked around, suddenly realizing that she hadn't seen Fluff since she got back. "Mom, where's Fluff? She didn't go out, did she?" Ella asked anxiously.

Her mom looked surprised. "But she has her cat flap now, Ella. She's allowed outside! I saw her playing in the yard earlier."

Ella looked worried. "I told her not to. I was scared she'd get lost in the snow again. I suppose it was silly to think she wouldn't go out."

"I don't think you need to worry, Ella," her mom said reassuringly. Fluff's not a baby anymore. I know she's still tiny, but she *has* grown! She's definitely old enough to be out there."

"But it's been snowing really hard today, Mom! And Fluff *always* comes back to see me when I get home from school. Always." Ella got up to peer out the kitchen window. "The snow's really deep in the yard. She could easily have gotten confused about where she was going. Oh, why didn't I just lock the cat flap?"

"Ella, it's not fair to lock it, unless we really need to. Fluff wouldn't understand why she couldn't go out. She'd just get upset." But Ella's mom came to join her at the window. "You're right, though; it *is* odd that she isn't back yet. I wonder where she went."

"We should go out and look for her," Ella said, heading for the hallway to put all her outdoor things back on.

"Oh, Ella, no. I'm sure we don't need to. Sit down and finish your hot chocolate. Honestly, Fluff was having a great time out there earlier. She was playing with the snowflakes. She probably just got too caught up with exploring. I'm sure she'll be home in a minute."

Ella trailed reluctantly back to the table. She knew Mom was right, but something was still nagging at her. Fluff had *never* missed meeting her before.

Ella's mom didn't sit back down, but stayed thoughtfully staring out the window. She wished she was as sure as she was trying to sound to Ella. She didn't think Fluff was lost, but she *was* worried. Fluff should have been back—was she hiding somewhere, waiting for the snow to stop? She just couldn't help feeling that it was an awfully cold day for a small kitten to be stuck outside....

Fluff stood up, her whiskers twitching. Usually hearing another cat would have made her fur stand on end, and she'd be wanting to fight and defend her territory. But there was something about that cry. She didn't think that the cat making that noise was going to be putting up much of a fight. She picked her way out of her blanket nest and stood still, listening carefully. She'd been so sleepy when she heard the meowing that she wasn't quite sure where it had come from.

There it was again. So quiet. So weak. Fluff listened anxiously. The other cat wasn't in this room; she was almost sure. She picked her way over the garbage and fallen bricks and peered through the doorway.

The house was tiny, with only
two rooms. The inner
room was full of broken
furniture, and Fluff leaped
up onto an old chair
to try and see what
was happening.
The room was
silent, and she
looked around
worriedly. She
was sure she
hadn't imagined it. Although—the
meow had seemed to be part of her
dream at first.... No! There it was
again. The cry was coming from a
battered cupboard on the other side of
the room. Fluff wove her way carefully
through the junk and nosed at the door.

71

It swung open slightly, and cautiously she stuck her head inside.

Staring back at her out of the gloom was an enormous pair of green eyes.

The meow came again, and Fluff watched in horror as a tiny white kitten struggled to its feet, desperately trying to reach her.

The kitten could hardly stand, and at once Fluff jumped into the cupboard, nosing the little creature gently. She towered over it. This kitten was much too young to be on her own! She looked as though she was only just old enough to eat food, rather than milk from her mother. Where *was* her mother? Fluff could smell that at least one other cat had been here. Maybe this was where the kitten had been born. Cats often choose odd places to have their kittens—*she* had been born in a stable, and the horse it belonged to hadn't been happy at all.

But the mother cat's scent was fading. *This kitten has been alone for a while,* Fluff thought. She had to be starving. She was nuzzling hopefully at Fluff, as though she thought Fluff might have brought her some food, but eventually she gave up and collapsed again. The cupboard was lined with rags, like the nest Fluff had made, and the white kitten lay down, curling herself up tight. She looked cold. Fluff lay down gently, curling herself around the kitten, like her own mother used to snuggle up to Fluff and her brothers and sisters.

The kitten meowed again, an even smaller sound this time, but she sounded satisfied. Fluff purred comfortingly. *Go to sleep. Maybe we can find your mother,* she thought. But she had a horrible feeling that the kitten's mother was far away. Somehow they'd been separated.

Fluff rested her head gently next to

the little white ears, watching anxiously as the kitten twitched her way to sleep. Fluff's tummy rumbled, but at least she'd had breakfast, which was more than she guessed the kitten had. She could feel the tiny body warming up, and her own eyes began to close.

Curled around each other, the two cats slept, alone in the snowy night.

Chapter Five
Searching for Fluff

Ella got up at six the next morning. It was still completely dark, but she didn't care. She felt as though she hadn't slept at all, though she figured she must have. All her plans for a weekend of fun in the snow were gone—Fluff still wasn't back. Ella went downstairs, put on her winter boots, coat and scarf, and unlocked the back door.

The cat flap swung open as she went out, and she felt like kicking it. She *should* have locked it, no matter what Mom said. She would rather have a grumpy Fluff than no Fluff at all.

Out in the backyard, the snow looked even deeper. There must have been another big snowfall during the night. Ella shivered. It was really freezing, even wrapped up as she was. She sighed. The yard looked so beautiful, all white with patches of green and icicles hanging from the branches. It was like a Christmas card—there was even a robin perched on the fence, looking at her hopefully to see if she was about to put crumbs out. Ella smiled a very small smile. If Fluff had been here, she would have been jumping up and down under the fence trying to get him. But all that proved was that Fluff definitely *wasn't* anywhere in the yard. Tucking her hands under her arms to try and keep them warm, Ella walked down the path—or rather, where she thought the path should be, since she couldn't see it at all.

"Fluff! Fluff, come on. Breakfast!" she called, trying to sound cheerful.

She stared around the yard, willing a stripy little furry body to come shooting out of the bushes. Then her heart leaped as she saw something moving at the far end of the yard. "Fluff!" she squeaked delightedly, running toward her. "Oh, Fluff, you had me so worried. You bad cat! I thought I'd lost you again. Oh!" Ella stopped suddenly as the strange cat stared up at her in surprise. It looked rather offended—as though it had been minding its own business, going for a morning walk, and suddenly it was being chased by a screaming girl. It twitched its tail irritably, then strolled on over the snow in a very dignified and haughty way, deliberately ignoring Ella.

79

"Sorry...," Ella whispered after it. She knew it was silly to apologize to a cat, but it seemed to be the kind of cat who would expect her to. Now that she could see it clearly, it didn't even look much like Fluff. It was much bigger, and its tabby coat was more spotted than striped. Trying not to cry, she trudged back to the house.

Her parents were in the kitchen making breakfast. They were both dressed, which wasn't normal for a Saturday. Usually everyone got up slowly, enjoying the weekend.

"Any luck?" Ella's dad asked. "We heard you calling."

Ella shook her head.

"I thought I saw her," she said miserably. "But it was another cat."

"I'm sure she's just waiting for the snow to stop," Ella's mom said briskly. "She'll be back soon. Sit down and have some breakfast, Ella."

"The snow *has* stopped," Ella pointed out, as she perched on the very edge of a chair. "So why isn't she back?"

Ella's parents glanced at each other with raised eyebrows, and she glared at them. "You're not taking this seriously!" she burst out. "Fluff's lost! I'm sure she is. We have to go and look for her."

Her dad sighed. "I have to say, I'm surprised she isn't back. She's never stayed out this long before, has she?"

Ella's mom nodded reluctantly. "I guess not. I've just been hoping she'd pop through the cat flap any minute, but maybe we should go and look for her. We should probably start by asking the neighbors if they've seen her."

Ella leaped up from the chair, heading for the door.

"Ella!" her mom yelled after her. "It's six thirty! On a Saturday! You can't go and wake up the entire street. Eat some breakfast first."

A couple of hours later, Ella and her parents had asked up and down the street, but no one had seen Fluff. Everyone was upset to hear she was missing—many of the neighbors had said how sweet she was, and how she often came up to be petted. Ella's parents had asked people to keep an eye out and check that she wasn't shut in any garages or sheds.

"Mrs. Jones's curtains are open now," Ella pointed out, as they trudged back up the street. "Can we go and ask her? Fluff loves her yard. She spends a lot of time watching the fish in her pond."

"Yes, we might as well," her mom agreed.

Mrs. Jones was horrified. "Poor thing," she said, sounding really worried. "It's so cold out. Oh, Ella, I'm sorry," she added, seeing Ella's eyes fill with tears. "You must be beside yourself, especially with her being lost before. I'm sure she'll turn up. She's such a bright little thing. She's probably just found herself a nice warm spot to wait out the storm. I'm sure she'll be back soon."

"Have you been out in your yard?" Ella said, sniffing. "She might be by your pond."

"The pond's frozen," Mrs. Jones replied. "I saw her looking at it yesterday, and she seemed very confused." She shook her head. "I don't think she's out there now, Ella, but you're welcome to go and check." She held the door open. "Why don't you all come in and have a cup of tea. You must be freezing."

She led the way into the kitchen and unlocked her back door for Ella to go out. Ella's parents sat down gratefully. They were just sipping the tea when Ella dashed back in, tears streaming down her face.

"Ella! What is it?" her mom asked, leaping up. "What's happened? Is Fluff—?"

Gulping, Ella stretched out her hand and laid something small and wet on the table next to the teacups.

It was Fluff's collar.

Fluff woke up as a cold wind cut through the door to the cupboard and made her twitch her ears uneasily. It took a few moments for her to figure out where she was, then she looked down worriedly at the white kitten. She was curled into a tiny ball, right up against Fluff's tummy, and she was deeply asleep. Fluff licked her gently, and she laid her ears back but didn't wake up. Fluff knew that she had to try and find her way home. Ella would be desperate, and the longer she left it, the harder it would be to find any tracks to help her get back. And she was starving! She'd missed her breakfast. That made her feel guilty, though—who knew when the younger kitten had last had anything to eat!

Fluff eyed her thoughtfully. She hadn't

sounded hungry last night. Was she so weak that she'd forgotten to be hungry? That was bad, very bad. Fluff needed to get home right away, and the little one had to wake up and come, too. Fluff nosed her firmly, and she gave a faint, complaining meow, then opened her green eyes and stared accusingly at Fluff.

Fluff licked her again, apologetically, then butted her in the chest to make her stand up. The kitten meowed miserably and tottered to her feet. Fluff stared at her, suddenly realizing that even now that she was warmed up, this tiny creature was not going anywhere. Fluff had found it almost impossible to stagger through the snow the day before—and this kitten was very weak!

But what should Fluff do?

89

She didn't want to leave the kitten behind, either. Helplessly, she watched as the little white cat gave another feeble meow and slumped back down again. No, she certainly wasn't coming on an expedition through the snow. Fluff would just have to go and find Ella and bring her back to help. The wailing wind had died down now, leaving an eerie silence, and Fluff thought the snow must have stopped. She would be able to see where she was going. She felt better now that she had made a decision, and she nosed her way out of the cupboard and across the room. She wanted to find some of the rags of blanket she had curled up in yesterday. The kitten wasn't as cold now, but without Fluff to keep her warm, she would quickly get cold again. Dragging the blanket back with her teeth, she wrapped it around the kitten.

A tiny purr rumbled through the scrap of white fur, making Fluff feel even more determined. She had to find help. Giving the kitten one last worried glance, she pushed the cupboard door with her nose to keep the cold out, and set off.

Fluff peered cautiously out of the hole in the front door and shivered. The snow was even deeper now, but at least it seemed frozen solid. She stepped out and looked helplessly around. Which way should she go? She had no idea. Even if she'd been able to remember which way she'd come, it all looked different now. Even the smells were covered in snow. She took a few uncertain steps, hoping to recognize something soon.

Then, to her horror, Fluff noticed snowflakes spiraling down. More snow! She looked up, hoping it would be just a light shower, but the sky was full of them, falling thickly down toward her. She needed to get back under cover fast—she knew from yesterday that there was no point in trying to go anywhere in this. But maybe she had time to find some food, before the storm got too heavy. Fluff looked around hopefully, but only saw trees. No good.

Hurrying back into the little house, she noticed something she hadn't seen in the dark the evening before. A battered old bag, lying by the door. Eagerly, Fluff clawed at it, retrieving a foil-wrapped packet. Ham sandwiches!

They didn't smell very fresh, but she was in no position to be fussy, and neither was the kitten.

The kitten did *not* want to be woken up again. Fluff had to swipe her on the nose to make her sit up and take notice of the food. She sniffed at it reluctantly, too tired to bother, but Fluff knew the kitten had to eat. She bit off a tiny piece of ham, and then nudged it against the kitten's mouth until she opened it to protest. As the taste of the food hit her tongue, she brightened a little, swallowing it down, and looked hopefully at Fluff for more. Fluff bit off some more pieces, gulping a few down herself. The kitten managed several mouthfuls, then curled up to sleep again.

Fluff watched her, feeling relieved. Surely the food would help her! She devoured the rest of the sandwich, then tucked herself back around the kitten. There didn't seem to be much else to do but sleep, so she slept.

It was much, much colder when she woke again. She was shivering, even wrapped up in their blanket nest. The kitten wasn't. She was completely still, and for an awful moment Fluff thought she wasn't even breathing.

There was a tiny snuffle of breath, but it was so shallow—as though the kitten could hardly be bothered. When Fluff nudged her, she wouldn't wake up. She was too cold.

Fluff stood up. The cold seemed to be inside her now, a freezing fear that she wouldn't be able to save this little one. The kitten had no one to help her but Fluff. Even if it was still snowing, she had go, *now*, and find Ella, and bring her back.

Chapter Six
The Rescue Mission

Fluff staggered through the snow, her paws aching with the cold. Every so often she had to stop and rest, taking in deep, shaky breaths of the freezing cold air, and each time it was harder to set off again. But she couldn't give up. She was desperate to find Ella now. If Fluff could just keep going, surely she would find her soon, and she'd be home and warm, and Ella would be able to help the snow-white kitten. She plowed on, trying not to think of the cold, just imagining the big bowl of tuna fish that Ella would give her....

"Ella, sweetheart, we have to go back home now. It's turned really cold—it's not good for us to be out in this for so long." Ella's mom was looking really anxious.

"But Mom, Fluff's out in it!" Ella cried. "And she's tiny and she isn't wearing a great big coat and boots and a hat and—"

"Yes, yes, I know." Mom sighed. "Just a little longer, then. We've been up and down the street twice now, though, and I don't know where else to look."

"What about that little wooded area that backs up to the yards further down the street?" Ella's dad suggested.

"Well, yes, I suppose she could have gotten in there," Mom agreed doubtfully. "It's worth a try."

"There's an alley around the corner; we can get in that way." Dad strode off, with Ella trotting beside him.

They were a few steps in among the trees when Mom held Ella back. "I'm not sure this is a good idea after all," she told Ella. "The snow must have blown right in here. It's really deep, and there's bound to be tree roots and things hidden under the snowdrifts. You could break an ankle."

"Mmmm." Ella's dad looked thoughtful. "You're right. Maybe we should poke a branch into the snow to make sure we aren't about to fall into anything dangerous."

Ella wasn't listening. Letting go of her dad's arm, she took a shaky step forward and crouched down. Her parents watched in amazement as a tiny gray shape staggered toward them through the gloomy, snow-filled woods. Ella was crying, tears spilling down her face without her even noticing.

Fluff put on a burst of speed and shot into Ella's arms, curling her head joyfully in under Ella's chin, and purring with relief and happiness. She'd found Ella. She was back. She was safe.

For a few moments she allowed herself to enjoy being petted and cuddled and told how brave she was, and how naughty she was to go running off in the snow. Then she wriggled herself out from Ella's tight embrace, putting her paws against Ella's chest and meowing urgently.

"What's the matter?" Ella looked confused. Fluff had seemed so happy to see them, but now it was obvious that she wanted something.

Fluff struggled out of Ella's arms and jumped lightly down, looking back up at Ella and meowing again. *Follow me!* she was saying, as clearly as she could. She trotted a few paces back into the woods, and looked back at Ella pleadingly.

"What's she doing?" Dad asked. "Fluff, that's not the way home. Come on!"

"She wants us to follow her," Ella said firmly. "Look, she's calling us." And she set off after Fluff, who bounded ahead delightedly, all her tiredness gone. Only a few moments before, she had felt as though she was going to drop down in the snow and sleep. She had been struggling through the drifts for more than an hour, trying to find any signs of the way home. But now that she was back with Ella, she had a surge of new energy.

"Ella, be careful!" her mom called. "Don't trip over any fallen branches!" Ella's parents scrambled after them. They had no idea where they were going, but it was clear that Fluff was trying to get them to follow her to wherever she was headed. Anyone could see that. Every so often she would turn around to check that they were still with her, then head off again, following her paw prints purposefully back through the trees.

There it was! Fluff jumped through the door of the tiny house, popping her head back out to call to Ella. Ella crouched down to squeeze through the gap in the door after her.

"Ella, no!" her mom yelled. "You don't know what's in there!"

"It's okay, Mom," Ella called back. "I'm following Fluff. It's fine."

Her mother tried to catch up and stop her, worried that the old building might be falling down, but she slipped on the snow, falling onto her hands and knees just in time to see Ella disappearing into the building. Ella's dad stopped to help her up, and they skidded over to look through the window.

Fluff wove her way hurriedly through the house, still calling to Ella to follow.

"I'm coming, I'm coming, Fluff! I can't fit underneath all this stuff like you can!" Ella puffed, scrambling over a pile of old sofa cushions. "I wish I knew what you were trying to show me." She realized that Fluff had stopped next to an old cupboard that was jammed up against the far wall. She was peering around the door, her body tense, nervous, almost scared—as though she wasn't sure what she was going to find.

Ella walked quietly up to Fluff and knelt behind her, but she couldn't see what Fluff was looking at. Suddenly, some of the stiffness went out of Fluff's spine, and she reached gently into the cupboard. She backed carefully out,

carrying something in her mouth—
something large. She dropped it in
Ella's lap, and it was only as Fluff sat
back and gazed hopefully up at her that
Ella realized what it was. Fluff had just
given her a kitten! She had pulled it out
of the cupboard like a magic trick.

"Fluff! It's a kitten! Where did you—?"

Fluff meowed urgently at her, and Ella looked more closely. She petted the tiny white head, and saw that the little creature didn't stir. She gave Fluff an anxious look, her heart thudding with nervousness. Fluff looked back up at her lovingly.

"I don't know," Ella said worriedly. "She's so little and weak, Fluff. I—I'm not even sure she's still breathing." She stood up, cradling the tiny furry ball gently. "Come on. We need to get her to a vet." Very carefully she wrapped the kitten in her scarf and tucked the package inside her jacket. She wasn't sure she could climb over all that junk carrying her.

Ella's parents were calling her as they

headed back, and her dad was starting to pull away the boards blocking the door.

"Ella! There you are!" he said angrily as she crouched to go through the hole. "What have you been doing? You should never have gone in there; what have we told you about playing in dangerous places like that?"

"I wasn't playing, Dad!" Ella said indignantly. "Look!" And she opened her jacket to show them her tiny passenger. "Fluff found her. But I'm not sure—" Her voice wobbled. "I can't see her breathing," she whispered, tears stinging the corners of her eyes.

"Let me see." Her dad lifted the kitten out, and she lay floppy and lifeless in his big hands. He was silent for an awful, long moment. "She is. But just barely.

Come on—we need to get home right now and call the vet. We need to tell them we have an emergency coming in."

Ella had been to the vet before to take Fluff to have all her vaccinations, but this time there was no hanging around in the reception area. She and her parents raced in, Ella cradling the kitten, and were rushed immediately into an exam room. It was the same vet who'd taken care of Fluff before, and she smiled, recognizing Ella.

"The receptionist said you'd found a stray kitten?" she asked, gently taking the scarf-wrapped bundle from Ella.

Ella nodded. "She's so tiny, and she's barely breathing," she explained. "It wasn't really us that found her, though. It was Fluff."

"We think she must have been

112

abandoned by her mother," Ella's dad put in. "Fluff and Ella found her in an old house in some woods near us."

The vet nodded thoughtfully. "She looks about three or four weeks old to me. Only just old enough to survive without her mother. She's very weak—I think she's had a couple of days on her own in the cold. I'm going to put her on a drip to get some food into her, and we'll put her in an incubator to get her nice and warm." She smiled, looking at Ella's anxious face. "I think you found her just in time. I can't promise, but it looks to me as if she's just cold and hungry, nothing worse. You might even be able to take her home in a couple of hours." She started to get the equipment she needed.

"Oh, that's fantastic!" Ella squeaked, not noticing that Mom and Dad looked a little shocked. "That's really good, because I don't think Fluff will understand where she is. She looked so upset when we drove off. She was watching us through the window—"

"Ella, Ella, hang on," Mom interrupted. "We don't know who this kitten belongs to. And we already have Fluff, so I'm not sure we can—"

"Mom!" Ella was horrified. "We have to take her home! Fluff saved her— what are you going to tell Fluff if we go back without her?"

Dad looked thoughtful. "Didn't the people who moved from that house down the street a few days ago have a white cat? I'm sure I remember seeing one around. Was she pregnant? Maybe she decided to have her kittens in that house. Cats do that sometimes, don't they?" he asked the vet. "Find strange places to have their kittens?"

The vet nodded. "It's all about wanting to be private, and keeping the kittens safe. If her owners were moving, she might not have liked all the mess of packing up at home." She was laying the white kitten in what looked like a fish tank. "This has a heat mat to warm her up gently," she explained. "I'll take her into a room in the back when she's settled."

Ella peered through the plastic side. The kitten looked really cozy, but that gave her a horrible thought. "What happened to the other kittens?" she asked worriedly. "Do you think they're outside somewhere? There was only this little one in the cupboard."

"Maybe the mother carried them back to the house," the vet said thoughtfully. "Or maybe she only had the one. That happens sometimes, and it would mean that it wasn't too obvious she was going to have kittens. Her owners might not have known."

Mom looked sad. "So they took her with them and left the kitten behind."

"Yes, she might have had to go home for some food. Thank goodness for Fluff," the vet said, smiling.

Mom sighed, and shook her head. "I guess you're right, Ella. After what Fluff did, we have to take this one home, too." Then she smiled. "I should have known it wouldn't stop with one!"

"You mean we can keep her?" Ella asked, hopping up and down. "Really?"

Her dad grinned. "Why not. It took forever to put in that cat flap, so we might as well use it…. Ooof!" he gasped as Ella hurled herself at him for a hug.

"Thank you, thank you, thank you! I can't wait to tell Fluff!"

Back at home, Fluff was sitting anxiously on the windowsill. She didn't quite understand where Ella and the kitten had gone, but Ella had whispered that they were taking care of her. She stared out at the snowy street, watching for the car, waiting for Ella. As they pulled up in front of the house, she jumped up with her paws scratching on the glass, meowing excitedly. Where was the kitten?

Ella carefully got out of the car, and Fluff watched in relief as she walked slowly up the path, cradling the kitten. Fluff was there waiting as they opened the door, weaving affectionately around Ella's ankles, then leading Ella to the kitchen and her too-big basket. She watched as Ella carefully set the kitten down on the red cushion, then she stepped in and curled herself around the white kitten lovingly.

The kitten, who'd been fast asleep ever since they left the vet, opened one eye sleepily and looked up at Fluff.

"Prrrp," she chirped, and a very small bright-pink tongue shot out and licked Fluff's nose. Then she went back to sleep.

Fluff looked down at her, and then back at Ella, who was crouched next to the basket, watching.

Ella reached over to scratch Fluff under the chin. "What should we call her?" she wondered, looking at the kitten's white fur, snuggled next to

Fluff's tabby coat. "How about Snowy? She *is* our snow rescue kitten."

Fluff yawned and stretched a little in agreement.

Ella grinned, watching the two of them nap. "It looks like we were right to buy a big basket after all!"

Available now:

Pet Rescue Adventures

Alone in the Night

by HOLLY WEBB

Jasmine is thrilled when her neighbors ask her to cat-sit while they go away for Christmas. Now she'll be able to spend her entire vacation with their beautiful cat named Star.

Star loves playing with Jasmine, and soon the pair are inseparable. But what Jasmine doesn't know is that Star has a secret. Although it is cold and dark outside, the time has come for Star to leave Jasmine and her warm, safe home and find a place to hide. But where should she go?

Available now:

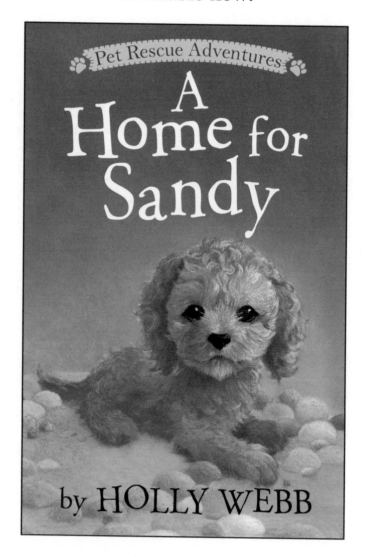

Pet Rescue Adventures

A Home for Sandy

by HOLLY WEBB

Anna has been worried about feeling lonely on vacation with only her baby sister to play with. So she is delighted when she meets some new friends on the beach. And when a beautiful puppy, Sandy, joins in their games, it looks like this could be the best summer ever!

It's been such a long time since Sandy had an owner. Then she meets Anna, and she doesn't feel so alone anymore. But will Anna be able to give Sandy the home she's been looking for?

Available now:

Pet Rescue Adventures

Teddy in Trouble

by HOLLY WEBB

Katy can't believe it when her parents agree to let her have a dog. And when she meets a lively puppy named Teddy, she's sure her family will fall in love with him, just as she has.

But her sister, Diana, is worried about how their cat, Misty, will react to the new arrival. Katy thinks they'll get used to each other, but things don't go as planned. Every time Teddy tries to play with Misty, he upsets her and gets into trouble. Teddy is so sad. Why doesn't Misty want to be friends?

HOLLY WEBB

Holly Webb started out as a children's book editor, and wrote her first series for the publisher she worked for. She has been writing ever since, with more than 100 books to her name. Holly lives in England with her husband, three young sons, and several cats who are always nosing around when she is trying to type on her laptop.

For more information
about Holly Webb visit:

www.holly-webb.com
www.tigertalesbooks.com